Parent's Introduction

We Both Read is the first series of books designed to invite parents and children to share the reading of a story by taking turns reading aloud. This "shared reading" innovation, which was developed in conjunction with early reading specialists, invites parents to read the more sophisticated text on the left-hand pages, while children are encouraged to read the right-hand pages, which have been written at one of three early reading levels.

Reading aloud is one of the most important activities parents can share with their child to assist their reading development. However, *We Both Read* goes beyond reading *to* a child and allows parents to share reading *with* a child. *We Both Read* is so powerful and effective because it combines two key elements in learning: "showing" (the parent reads) and "doing" (the child reads). The result is not only faster reading development for the child, but a much more enjoyable and enriching experience for both!

Most of the words used in the child's text should be familiar to them. Others can easily be sounded out. An occasional difficult word will be first introduced in the parent's text, distinguished with **bold lettering**. Pointing out these words, as you read them, will help familiarize them to your child. You may also find it helpful to read the entire book aloud yourself the first time, then invite your child to participate on the second reading. Also note that the parent's text is preceded by a "talking parent" icon: ⬭ ; and the child's text is preceded by a "talking child" icon: ⬭ .

We Both Read books is a fun, easy way to encourage and help your child to read — and a wonderful way to start your child off on a lifetime of reading enjoyment!

We Both Read: Ben and Becky Get a Pet

Text Copyright © 1998 by Sindy McKay
Illustrations Copyright © 1998 by Meredith Johnson
All rights reserved

We Both Read™ is a trademark of Treasure Bay, Inc.

Published by Treasure Bay, Inc.
50 Horgan Ave., Suite 12
Redwood City, CA 94061 USA

PRINTED IN SINGAPORE

Library of Congress Catalog Card Number: 98-60704

Hardcover ISBN 1-891327-06-2
Softcover ISBN 1-891327-10-0

FIRST EDITION

We Both Read™ Books
Patent Pending

Ben & Becky
Get a Pet

By Sindy McKay

Illustrated by Meredith Johnson

TREASURE BAY

This is a picture of my big sister and me.

My sister's name is Rebecca Elizabeth. But everyone calls her Becky.

My mom says Becky is a strong-willed and tenacious individual. I say, if there's something she wants, she usually gets it.

My name is Benjamin. But you can call me Ben.

Sometimes Becky and I get along. Most of the time we don't. But one time Becky and I wanted the same thing. And we worked together to get it.

Becky and I wanted a pet.

We asked our mom about it, but she said it was up to our dad. So Becky and I pestered him about a pet for almost a month.

Mom said she'd never seen two kids who were more persistent.

I think "persistent" is a good thing.

I told Dad I wanted a snake named "Killer." Becky said she wanted a cat named "Cupcake."

Dad said we would be lucky to get any pet at all.

"A pet is a big responsibility," he said. "Can you two be responsible?"

I crossed-my-heart-and-hoped-to-die that I could.

Becky promised "absolute reliability." (Mom says Becky has a large vocabulary. That means she uses a lot of big words that I don't always understand.)

"Okay," said Dad. "If you can be responsible, then you can get a pet."

YES!!! Becky and I were so happy that we hugged!

But not for very long.

Dad, Becky, and I headed for the mall and I said I was going to get the biggest, meanest-looking snake in the world!

Becky said I was "delusional."

The mall security **guard** held the door open as we thundered in and made a beeline for the pet store.

The mall was full of people. But that didn't stop Becky and me! We ran to the pet store as fast as we could go.

The **guard** ran after us and told us to slow down!

We dashed into the store and there, inside a big glass terrarium, was the coolest, greenest, shiniest snake I'd ever seen! A real "Killer"!

I lifted him out and felt his smooth, dry skin. He wasn't at all **gross** and slimy like I thought he would be.

I took Killer over to Becky who was by the kittens. **"Gross!"** she said. "Why do you want a snake?"

I stuck Killer in her face and she screamed!

That's why I want a snake.

Becky ran off to tattle to Dad.

"Da-ad! Ben wants a repulsive reptile. Please inform him we are getting a kitten."

I held Killer up to Dad. "Come on, Dad. **Admit** it! He's awesome!" Killer's tongue darted out to say hello then he slithered up my arm and curled around my shoulder.

Dad had to **admit** it — Killer was cool.
"But," he said, "the pet is for both of you.
So your sister has to like it, too."

And Becky did not like Killer.

Dad had to run some errands in the mall, so he told us to stay at the pet store and make a decision about our pet. And it had to be a "mutual" decision.

There was only one thing to do. I had to convince Becky of the "coolness" factor of the snake on my **shoulder**.

"Killer is very cool," I told Becky. "His skin comes off. He has no ears. He eats rats. He's great. He's wonderful!"

Becky pointed to my **shoulder**. "He's gone."

It was true! Killer had slithered off my shoulder and disappeared! Becky and I began to **search** the store, but we couldn't find him anywhere!

Becky was so mad her eyes almost popped out of her head.

"Ben, you are soooo irresponsible! Now Dad is *never* going to let us get a pet."

Becky was right. We had to find Killer. Or Dad would not let us get *any* pet.

I started to **search** the store again. I just had to find him!

Suddenly Becky shrieked and pointed toward the wall.
"There he is, Ben! Stop him before he gets away!"

But I wasn't worried. After all, not even a snake can go through a wall.

Unless, of course, there's a *hole* in the wall.

Killer slipped right through the hole in the wall.
I tried to go after him, but I was much too big.
"Great," said Becky. "Now we'll *never* find him!"
"Yes, we will," I said. But I didn't know how.

Suddenly we heard a bloodcurdling scream from the music store.

"See? I told you we would find him."

Becky and I raced next door and found a saleslady standing on top of the counter, screaming. She stopped to ask, "May I help you?"

We told her we were looking for a snake. She pointed to Killer. Then she started to scream again.

I told Becky to stay by the door so he couldn't get away. Then I ran over to grab him.

I missed.

Killer headed for the door at super-sonic speed!

"Quick! Grab him!" I yelled at Becky.

But no way was she going to grab a "repulsive reptile."

Besides, she was nowhere near the door. She was on the counter with the saleslady, screaming her guts out!

So I ran out the door after Killer. I spotted him crawling into a candy store. I started to run in after him. Then suddenly Becky pushed me to the ground!

She slapped her hand over my mouth and pointed. Standing near a jar of licorice was the mall security guard.

Inside the jar of licorice was Killer.

We held our breaths as the guard reached for the licorice jar.

Lucky for Killer, he decided on a jawbreaker instead.

The guard left and I shouted, "Quick, Becky! Grab Killer!"

Becky shouted back, "Are you crazy? I will *never* grab a snake!"

While we were fighting, Killer went back out into the mall.

Becky and I ran after him and discovered that the mall was really crowded. We kept bumping into people as we searched for Killer. I bumped into a guy with a hot dog and totally freaked when I saw his hot dog moving!

Then I realized — it was no hot dog.

It was Killer.

The man saw Killer too. He threw his hot dog into the air. It came down on top of a lady's head. Killer crawled out and went down her neck.

Boy, did she scream!

Now *everyone* knew there was a snake in the mall and things went totally crazy.

People ran into stores! Out to their cars! Up onto benches! Into the **trash cans**! Becky called it "mass hysteria," and "utter panic."

All because of a little green snake.

Becky and I looked around. The crowd was gone now — except for the people in the **trash cans**. It should have been easy to find Killer.

It *should* have been. But it wasn't.

"Let's just forget it, Becky. We're never going to find him."

Becky scowled. "Don't be such a pessimist, Ben. No repulsive reptile is going to get the best of *me*!"

"But how will we find him?"

Becky said all we had to do was listen.

And Becky was right. Because just then
we heard a scream. It came from the dress
shop across the way.

A screaming lady ran out the door.
Becky and I ran in to look for Killer.

I spotted Killer scooting under a dressing room door so I scooted in behind him — just in time to see the lady inside put on her belt. Only it wasn't a belt she was putting on.

It was Killer.

I was so excited I shouted, "There's my *snake*!"

I grabbed for Killer. But someone grabbed *me* first.
It was the mall guard.

"You're in big trouble, young man."

He said it wasn't nice to scare people by saying
there is a snake in the store. I told him there really was
a snake in the store. But I don't think he believed me.

The guard was pulling me out of the store when Becky ran up and tried to explain things. But he didn't believe her either.

The only way to make him believe us was to show him the snake. And to do that, Becky had to catch the "repulsive reptile."

The guard was right. I was in BIG trouble.

"Don't worry, Ben," Becky said. "I'll catch him." And off she ran to find Killer.

This would be the hardest thing Becky would ever do.

Becky told me later that it took "every ounce of courage in her whole entire body" to pick up Killer, but that she was surprised when she felt his smooth, cool skin.

Maybe he wasn't such a "repulsive reptile" after all.

Becky ran over to the guard with Killer in her hand. Boy, was I happy! She showed the guard the snake.

He fainted.

I think he finally believed us.

"Let's not tell Dad about any of this, "Becky suggested as we hurried back to the pet store. "No need to upset him, you know."

But we did tell Dad about it. All of it. And we admitted that a pet was a pretty big responsibility — one that maybe we weren't ready for yet.

We waited for Dad to yell at us. But he didn't yell. He smiled! Then he took something from behind his back.

"A big pet can be a lot of work. So maybe we should start out small."

 "Omigosh, it's a hamster," Becky squealed as she took the little fur ball from Dad. "He's the cutest thing in the whole entire world!"

"He's not cute," I said. "He's a Killer!"

And that's the story of how my sister and I got a pet.

The next time we went to the mall, I looked for the guard. I told him I was sorry about what happened with the old Killer. I asked him if he wanted to meet the new Killer. He said, "NO THANKS!!"

I wonder why.